Why Do Grown-ups Have All the Fun?

by MARISABINA RUSSO

Greenwillow Books, New York

Printed in Hong Kong by South China Printing Co.
First Edition   1 2 3 4 5 6 7 8 9 10
The full-color art work, gouache paintings, were mechanically
separated and reproduced in four colors. The text typeface is
Avant Garde Book, and the display type is Tabasco Medium.

Library of Congress Cataloging-in-Publication Data

Russo, Marisabina.
Why do grown-ups have all the fun?
Summary: When Hannah is in bed unable to sleep,
she imagines all the fun the grown-ups are having—
doing all the things she herself likes to do.
[1. Bedtime—Fiction]   I. Title.
PZ7.R9192Wh 1987   [E]   86-4644
ISBN 0-688-06625-9
ISBN 0-688-06626-7 (lib. bdg.)

For my mother,
and Eunice and Whit

One night Hannah just could not fall asleep.
Neither could her doll Aggie.
Hannah was sure that her mother and father
were doing something wonderful.
"Why do grown-ups have all the fun?"
she said to Aggie.

"Right this very minute I bet Mama and Daddy are eating ice cream with sprinkles and marshmallows," said Hannah.

Hannah took Aggie and tiptoed down the hall. She peeked into the living room. Her mother was sewing. Her father was reading. Hannah and Aggie tiptoed back to bed.

Hannah still could not fall asleep.

Neither could Aggie.

"I bet Mama made a pot of play dough. Right this very minute Mama and Daddy are squishing it and rolling it and cutting it," said Hannah.

Hannah took Aggie and tiptoed down the hall.
She peeked into the living room. Her mother and
father were folding clean sheets together.
Hannah and Aggie tiptoed back to bed.

Hannah still could not close her eyes.
"I'll be up all night," said Hannah.
"I'll never fall asleep as long as Mama
and Daddy are having all the fun."

"I bet Mama and Daddy built a big tower with blocks and they are getting ready to crash the whole thing down," said Hannah. "And then they are going to eat popcorn."

Hannah took Aggie and tiptoed down the hall.

She peeked into the living room.

Her mother was writing a letter.

Her father was doing a crossword puzzle.

"Mama, Daddy, I can't fall asleep.
Neither can Aggie," said Hannah.
"Do you want to come sit with us on the
couch for a while?" said her mother.

Hannah climbed up on the couch with Aggie.
She snuggled down between her mother and
father. Her mother went back to her letter.
Her father went back to his crossword puzzle.
It was very quiet.

Finally Hannah said, "Aggie is getting sleepy
now so we are going to bed."
"We'll come and tuck you both in," said her mother.
"See you in the morning," said Hannah.
And she went to sleep.